GARFIELD'S
Christmas Tales

Created by
JIM DAVIS

Written by Mark Acey and Jim Kraft

Designed and Illustrated by Mike Fentz

 Troll

Contents

GARFIELD'S SWEET DEAL

'Twas the day before Christmas, and Garfield, as usual, was nestled all snug in his bed. Suddenly, there was a loud, urgent knock at the door. Garfield glanced at the clock, then grunted and pulled his blanket over his head.

People are so inconsiderate, he thought. *How dare they make all this racket in the middle of the afternoon. And just when I was dreaming about eating all those Christmas cookies Jon baked.*

RAP! RAP! RAP! The knocking continued. Finally, Garfield crawled out of bed and answered the door. He was greeted by a strange little man with pointy ears who was jumping up and down and waving his hands.

"Who, or should I say what, are you?" inquired Garfield. "Some sort of munchkin?"

"My name's Bimple, and I'm Santa Claus's chief elf," gasped the man, still clearly agitated.

"Oh, you're Santa's elf, are you?" replied Garfield doubtingly. "How do I know you're not just a confused leprechaun?"

"Look, Lardball, I don't have time for this small talk. We have an emergency on our hands."

"Call 911, then," said Garfield as he headed toward the kitchen. "I'm about to have my hands full of Christmas cookies."

"You don't understand," pleaded Bimple, as he followed Garfield into the kitchen. "Last night Santa Claus was kidnapped at the North Pole by space aliens! They want him to make toys for their children. I stowed away on their spaceship to try to rescue Santa. We were on our way to outer space when the ship experienced engine trouble. The ship had to land in a field near your house to make repairs, and I sneaked away to find help. Please, you've got to help me save Santa!"

"That's quite a story," said Garfield. "Have you thought about selling it to the *National Tattler*? But seriously — assuming what you say is true — why should I risk my skin against an army of aliens?"

"Because children all over the world are looking forward to Santa Claus at this time of the year. Besides, if you don't help me, I'll make certain you get an exercise bike for Christmas."

"Enough said," replied Garfield. "It's time for this cat to act." Garfield thought intensely for a moment, then picked up a cookie. "I work better on a full stomach," he said. "I'd offer you one, Bimple, but then there would be one less for me."

Suddenly, Garfield was struck by an idea. He looked longingly at the plate of cookies. Their delectable jimmies, nuts, and chocolate made his mouth water. Finally, Garfield nodded his head.

"It will require the ultimate sacrifice on my part, but it just might do the trick."

"What's the plan?" asked the elf excitedly.

"It's simple, Bimple. We're going to exchange these cookies for Santa."

"That's a *terrible* idea," groaned Bimple. "Santa's worth a lot more than a few cookies."

"Never underestimate the power of food," said Garfield. "Anyway, it's worth a try."

Bimple quickly led Garfield, who was clutching the prized cookies, to the edge of the field where the spaceship had landed. Peering through the bushes, Garfield stared in amazement at the strange creatures. The aliens had triangular heads, floppy ears, huge stomachs, and three spindly legs.

"Yuk," whispered Garfield to Bimple. "Those aliens are even uglier than dogs. Although, I must admit, I admire their jelly bellies. Speaking of which — there's Santa!"

Santa Claus was standing next to the ship, imprisoned by a glowing force field. Summoning their courage, Garfield and Bimple approached the alien with the biggest stomach.

"I am Garfield, top cat of the planet Earth. This is Bimple, Santa's number-one elf."

"I am Moto, captain of the spaceship Regoob," replied the aliens' leader as his crew quickly surrounded Garfield and Bimple. "We hail from the planet Namok."

"Good, you speak English," said Garfield.

"Of course. We are advanced beings. We speak everything."

"Looks like you also *eat* everything," said Garfield. "I like that in an alien. Which brings me to my point. I have something here that may be much more valuable to you than old St. Nick."

Garfield handed Moto one of the Christmas cookies. The captain eyed it suspiciously, then started to stick it up his nose.

"No, you *eat* it," explained Garfield.

"That is what I am doing," said Moto as he shoved the cookie up his gaping nostril. Moto's face immediately broke into a grin.

"This is good!" he cried. "We do not have anything like this on our planet. The children will like this even better than toys."

"Exactly," agreed Garfield. "The best things in life are edible. These cookies are good because they're *sweet*. The children on Earth love sweet foods."

Moto tried to snatch the cookies, but Garfield whisked the plate behind his back.

"Not so fast," warned Garfield. "I'll give you the cookies — and tell you how to make more — if you release Santa and return him and Bimple to the North Pole."

"It is a deal," said Moto as he deactivated the force field. Garfield, in turn, reluctantly surrendered the cookies. And he taught the aliens how to bake more.

"The repairs have been made," said Moto. "We are ready for liftoff."

Before boarding the ship, Bimple and Santa thanked Garfield.

"You gave up your cookies so the children could be happy," said Santa. "That's a very noble thing to do. Perhaps you'll get something extra for Christmas this year."

"A large pizza with extra cheese would be nice," said Garfield. Santa and Bimple walked up the gangplank, then turned and waved good-bye. Moments later, the spaceship zoomed off toward the North Pole.

In the wee hours of Christmas morning, while Jon and Odie still lay fast asleep, Garfield leapt out of bed and hurried into the living room to see what Santa had brought him. But to Garfield's dismay, he found nothing. His stocking was empty and there were no new gifts under the tree.

I hope Santa's just running late, thought Garfield as he vainly searched the fireplace for presents. *Or what if those aliens broke their promise and never took him home?*

Suddenly, there was a rumbling in the chimney. Before Garfield could move, the rumble turned into a roar as thousands of colorful cookies cascaded down the chimney, engulfing him.

"How sweet it is!" whooped Garfield, frolicking in the cookies.

In the distance, Garfield heard a faint "Ho! Ho! Ho!" Then a large flat cardboard box landed at the bottom of the fireplace. Garfield opened it and found a freshly baked pizza with extra cheese.

Thanks, Santa. You really delivered, thought Garfield. *Now I have so many goodies, I can even share them with Jon and Odie. Well, maybe just a few.*

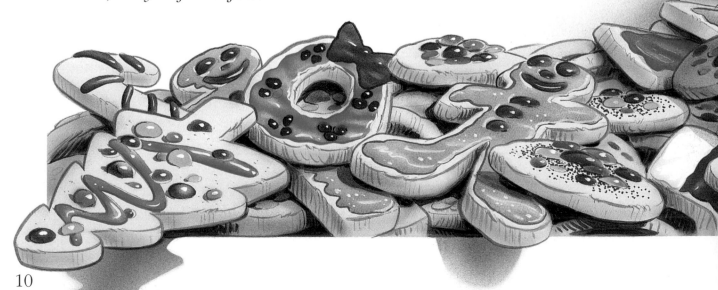

11

THE GREAT SNOWBALL FIGHT

The snow fell steadily on the Arbuckle farm.

"What could be better than spending Christmas in the country?" remarked Jon, taking a deep breath of the crisp winter air.

"Nothing, if you have hay for a brain," grumbled Garfield. "Personally, I'm bored out of my gourd."

"Let's shovel some snow and then chop some wood," suggested Jon. "That should get the ol' heart pumping."

"And the ol' back aching," added Garfield, starting to make his getaway. "If you need me, I'll either be raiding the henhouse or the refrigerator."

And with that, Garfield disappeared. Before long, he came to a fence that separated the Arbuckle property from a neighboring farm. A sign on the barn read: "U.S. Acres." Across the way, a pig, a rooster, and a duck were being bombarded with snowballs by three burly, surly hogs who had built a snow fort at the top of a hill. Amused, Garfield climbed over the fence for a better look.

Finally, a little entertainment, he thought, as snowballs walloped the rooster and the duck.

"Serves you right, rooster," heckled Garfield. "That's what you get for waking everyone up in the morning. Hey duck, you forgot to duck!"

But Garfield's taunting was short-lived. One of the hogs suddenly launched a soggy snow missile that landed right on Garfield's furry noggin! All of the farm animals shrieked with laughter. Garfield, of course, went ballistic.

"Why you no-good, slop-swilling swine! Nobody nails me and gets away with it. I'll carve you into pork chops and fry you up for my dinner!"

The barrage of snowballs stopped for a moment as the three horrible hogs grunted with glee and ran behind their fort.

"Don't let them give pork a bad name," pleaded a nearby pig as he, the rooster, and the duck approached the fence. "Hi, I'm Orson. These are my friends, Roy the rooster and Wade the duck. And, unfortunately, those three big bullies are my siblings, Mort, Wart, and Gort. Folks around here refer to them as the 'Grunt Brothers.'"

"Well, as far as I'm concerned, their name is mud," said Garfield. "As for me, Garfield's my name and revenge is my game. What's wrong with you guys, anyway? Why do you put up with those bloated mud monkeys?"

"What can we do?" stammered Wade. "I'm afraid we just have to live with it."

"You're afraid of everything — even water," snapped Roy, pointing to Wade's inner tube. "But for once the scaredy-duck is right. The Grunt Brothers are even meaner than they are ugly."

"They've been tormenting me all of my life," chimed in Orson. "We're lucky they only come around once in a while. We try to ignore them and hope they'll go away."

"Well, I'm not about to take this lying down," huffed Garfield, "although I could use a nap."

"Garfield's right," said Orson. "It's time we stood up to these bullies once and for all."

"I'll sound the battle cry!" whooped Roy, hoisting his trusty bugle. "Charge!"

"Bag the bugle, Dumb Cluck," said Garfield. "Let's use our heads for something other than targets. It's *our* brains versus *their* brawn. What we need is a plan."

"Garfield has a point," agreed Orson. "We can't out-muscle them; we have to out*smart* them. And I have an idea that just might work. In this story I was reading—"

"Was it a scary story?" interrupted Wade. "You know how I feel about scary stories."

"You'll have to excuse Wade," said Orson to Garfield. "As you can see, he's scared of his own shadow."

Wade immediately glanced over his shoulder to see if his shadow had sneaked up on him.

"Cut to the chase," demanded Garfield. "What's your plan?"

"I read this story where ancient Roman soldiers were trying to conquer a city that was surrounded by a big wall. They used a contraption that was kind of like a giant slingshot to hurl huge rocks over the wall. They called this device a 'catapult.'"

"Why is it called a 'catapult'?" asked Wade.

"I don't know," replied Orson. "But I do know that a catapult is the answer to our problem."

"How's that?" clucked Roy.

"Elementary, my dear rooster," interjected Garfield. "If we had a catapult, we could wipe out the Grunt Brothers and their fort with a humongous snowball."

"Exactly," echoed Orson. "Of course, we'll have to build our own catapult. And we'd better hurry. If I know my brothers, this lull won't last long."

Springing into action, the farm animals rounded up tools from the barn, along with some old wood, rope, and rubber strips. Garfield naturally supervised.

"Now nail the doohickey to the thingamajig," ordered Garfield. "And don't forget the whatchamacallit."

Finally, they were finished.

"Gentlemen, I give you our catapult," announced Orson proudly.

"Why *do* they call it a catapult?" asked Roy.

"I don't know," responded Orson. "I just hope it works."

"We still need a snowball," observed Wade.

"Not a snowball," said Garfield. "We want a snow BOULDER!"

With that, the gang started to make a gigantic snowball. Just as they finished, the Grunt Brothers resumed their attack.

"Look," cried Wade. "They're *baaaack*!"
The Grunt Brothers were now standing atop their fort, hurling snowballs and insults.

"What are you sissies doing? Building a big bad snowman to frighten us away?" hooted Mort, as his cohorts snorted and cavorted. "And what's that monstrosity you've got down there — an overgrown mousetrap?"

"I can't wait to squash those rude rubes," said Garfield. "Come on, let's arm the catapult."

It took all of their strength to hoist the snow boulder up onto the makeshift catapult.

"Good job!" gasped Garfield. "Now all we have to do is release this rope and launch this snow bomb right into their fort. Stand back!" he shouted. "Ready. Aim. Fire!"

But something was wrong. The snow boulder didn't budge.

"It's stuck!" yelled Orson. "The rope's caught."

"Quick," commanded Garfield. "You guys tilt the boulder while I climb up and untangle the rope."

Orson, Wade, and Roy prepared to push the enormous snowball. Garfield crouched precariously alongside it.

"One . . . two . . . three . . . PUSH!" exhorted Orson.

Adrenaline pumping, the farm animals not only tilted the snow boulder, but shoved it completely off the catapult, triggering a wild chain reaction. Garfield lost his balance and tumbled onto the spot vacated by the boulder. The rope sprang free, and Garfield — screaming at the top of his lungs — was propelled high into the air. Soaring across the field like a furry cannonball, the fat cat landed smack dab on the Grunt Brothers, smashing their snow fort to smithereens!

Rejoicing in triumph, Orson, Wade, and Roy ran across the field to where Garfield and the vanquished hogs lay in a dazed pile on the snow. As Orson looked over the scene, a smile suddenly appeared on his face.

"So," he remarked, "that's why they call it a *cat*apult!"

SANTA'S HUNGRY LITTLE HELPER

"Garfield, you and Odie stay away from these treats," ordered Jon as he placed a plate of cookies and a glass of milk near the Christmas tree. "They're for Santa to eat tonight."

"Did someone say 'eat'?" Garfield instantly awoke from his favorite Christmas dream of lasagna-flavored candy canes.

"See you boys in the morning," called Jon, heading upstairs to bed. "And remember, keep your paws off those cookies."

"No problem," replied Garfield, immediately lifting up the plate and pouring the cookies into his mouth.

Odie stared in disbelief.

"Hey, Jon said to keep our *paws* off the cookies," said Garfield. "He didn't say anything about our *jaws*. Now go get me a straw, and I'll polish off this milk."

Just then, something landed with a thud on the roof: Santa Claus!

"Uh oh!" said Garfield. "Santa will think we're a bunch of ingrates if he sees this empty plate. My angelic reputation will be ruined!"

The flustered feline ran to the kitchen and opened the refrigerator.

"There must be *something* suitable for the old guy in here. Let's see . . . prunes, anchovies, headcheese. Hmm, not exactly your standard Yuletide fare."

From above, footsteps could be heard. Santa was heading for the chimney!

Garfield panicked. At the very back of the fridge was a hard lump covered with wrinkled tinfoil. "Hey! What's a rock doing in the . . . no, wait!" Garfield unwrapped the mystery food and examined it. "It looks like last year's fruitcake."

The clever cat grinned with pride. "Fruitcake is Christmas food! Santa will love it!"

Odie whimpered doubtfully.

"Oh, who asked you, Eggnog Breath?" said Garfield.

Just as Garfield set the year-old fruitcake on the plate, something rustled in the fireplace. Santa was in the house!

"We'd better hide," Garfield suggested. He and Odie scurried to a dark corner of the room. "We might make the 'naughty' list if Santa sees us up past our bedtime."

A moment later, Santa appeared! His beard was snowy white. His eyes twinkled like stars. And there was something magical in the way he carried his huge sack of gifts without any effort at all. Garfield and Odie were entranced.

Santa was tiptoeing toward the Christmas tree when something seemed to distract him.

"Follow his eyes," Garfield whispered. "They're glued to the food."

Garfield was right. As soon as Santa spied the fruitcake, he rushed toward it, letting the sack slip from his shoulder.
"Ahh," Garfield sighed admiringly. "There's a man after my own heart. Or should I say 'stomach'?"

While the two pets watched, Santa lifted the fruitcake to his lips and . . . KRR-SNAP! A sound like cracking walnuts filled the room.

"Oh, no!" cried Garfield as he and Odie rushed from their hiding place to see what had happened.

It was a strange sight. There was Santa, with the intact fruitcake in one hand — and a pile of teeth in the other!

"Oh, Santa! It's all my fault," Garfield confessed guiltily. "That stale fruitcake I found broke all your teeth! You must hate me!"

To Garfield's amazement, Santa simply chuckled.

"These aren't real teeth," he said. "They're my dentures." Santa held out his hand for Garfield and Odie to see. "I've worn this same old set for years. Mrs. Claus kept saying they would break on me one day."

"So, you're not mad?" Garfield meekly inquired.

"Of course not," replied Santa with a toothless grin. "How could I be angry on Christmas Eve?"

This Nick really is *a saint*, thought Garfield.

"But I *am* sad," Santa admitted. "People all over the world have left treats for me tonight." As Santa spoke, all the jolly seemed to go right out of him. "Now that I can't eat, everyone will be terribly disappointed."

"Don't worry, Santa." Garfield was determined to make things right. "If it's teeth you need, then teeth you'll have!"

With that, Garfield and Odie began a furious search of the house. Garfield, as usual, started in the kitchen.

"Toaster, tongs, tangerines . . ." he said. "We've got everything but teeth!"

Garfield was about to give up when Odie came bounding in. It was a Christmas miracle: Odie had found some teeth!

"Why, I bet these will do just fine," Santa said, taking a pair of funny-looking dentures from Odie's mouth. "In fact," he added, after washing off Odie's slobber, "they're downright cute."

Santa tried them on. "A perfect fit!" he exclaimed. But as soon as he spoke, the teeth began to chatter.

"Wha-wha-wha-what's h-h-h-happening?" Santa stuttered.

"Oops!" Garfield yanked the teeth out. "These are *chattering* teeth!" he explained.

Undaunted, Odie offered another pair.

"*Vampire* teeth?" said Santa.

"Okay, so maybe Halloween *was* two months ago, but we're desperate!" Garfield stuffed the fangs into Santa's mouth. "Well?"

Santa smiled. He looked like the fattest Dracula ever.

"They feel okay," said Santa.

"That's good enough for me," said Garfield. "Why don't you take them for a test bite?" He handed Santa the fruitcake.

With a lick of his lips, Santa seized the slice and tried to munch. But all he could do was puncture two holes in the cake. Dismayed, Santa removed the vampire teeth. "We've tried everything," he sighed. "There's nothing to do but disappoint the whole world."

"Wait!" cried Garfield. "Maybe you can use *my* teeth!"

"Huh?" Both Santa and Odie were puzzled.

"Just look at these chompers." Garfield flashed his broadest smile. "My teeth can handle any snack in the world — and my appetite can handle *every* snack in the world."

Santa's jolly glow returned as he began to understand Garfield's plan. "If you come with me, then *you* can eat the goodies."

"Exactly!" Garfield piped. "Then everyone will be happy — especially my tummy."

"Let's go, then!" Santa urged. "I've got millions of homes to visit."

"And I've got millions of calories to consume," Garfield added.

In a minute, they were gone. Odie waved good-bye as Santa's reindeer took them into the crisp December air. And that night, nobody was disappointed. Especially not Garfield — who, in a small Italian village, finally got to eat the Christmas treat of his dreams: a lasagna-flavored candy cane!

THE RAT BEFORE CHRISTMAS

'Twas the night before Christmas, and there I was, stuck in a stinking rathole. Which wasn't surprising — after all, I am a rat. And usually I'm a happy rat. But that December I was depressed. I was sick of spending Christmas in the sewer. I mean, did you ever deck the halls with boughs of soggy broccoli? It grosses the Yuletide spirit right out of you.

So that Christmas Eve I said good-bye to the sewer and went in search of happier holidays. As soon as I hit the gutter, I started to feel better. The air was so fresh and cold I thought my lungs would have a heart attack. And all around me were the sights and sounds of the season: the colored lights, the carols, the busy shoppers, the guy trying to whack me with a snow shovel. Even at Christmas, people have a hard time showing goodwill toward vermin.

Having scurried for my life, I leaned against a mailbox post and caught my breath. It was getting late. Time to find a cozy spot to wait for Santa. I scanned the house in front of me: wreath on the door, blinking angels in the windows, no obvious signs of felines. I decided to check it out.

Getting in was easy. (Don't ask — it's a rat secret.) I sniffed around the kitchen. There were two empty food dishes on the floor: one for something named "Garfield," the other for "Odie." The "Garfield" dish was the size of a wading pool, so I figured Garfield must be a pet hippo or something. As for "Odie" — whatever he was, he was probably as goofy as his name.

Three stockings hung above the fireplace in the living room. One average-size stocking said "Jon." One oversize stocking said "Garfield." And one stocking hanging upside-down said "Odie." Obviously, Odie was not real bright. Obviously, Odie was a dog.

Candy canes and strings of popcorn dangled from the branches of the Christmas tree. A fruitcake glistened on the coffee table. I helped myself to some cookies I found beside the fireplace.

I had just inhaled the last cookie crumb when my rat radar lit up like my cousin Ed when he ate that toxic waste. I spun around. A fat orange-and-black cat was glaring at me from across the room. So Garfield wasn't a hippo after all, I realized. Though he did a pretty good imitation.

I dove for the Christmas tree. In two seconds I was battling an angel for room at the top.

The cat sauntered over to the tree. "If it isn't the Ghost of Christmas Pest," he declared. "You made two big mistakes, rat. First, you ate the cookies Jon left for Santa. Jon won't like that."

"And the second mistake?" I asked.

"You ate them before *I* could. And I *really* don't like that!"

"Well, excuse *me* for being hungry," I snapped.

"If you were hungry, why didn't you eat the fruitcake?" asked the cat.

"Oh, puh-lease," I replied. "Just because I eat garbage, that doesn't mean I'll eat *anything*."

"You've got me there," said the cat, with a grimace. "Fruitcake is about as tasty as rat pudding."

"You mean, you don't want to eat me?" I asked.

"Ugh! No way," the cat replied. "But I might slice you into hairy tinsel unless you leave right now."

"But it's Christmas Eve!" I argued.

"So go celebrate in the sewer!" he said, jerking his thumb toward the door.

I shook my head. "No. I like it here, and I'm staying. If you want me to go, you're going to have to throw me out." And just to show I was serious, I bounced an ornament off the fat cat's head.

"Ouch!" cried the cat. "That does it! I'm going to flush you back where you belong!"

With that he threw his hefty leg up on a branch and began to climb. What was I to do? I was trapped. Would I ever see the familiar slime of home?

Then, when the cat had nearly reached the top, the tree began to wobble like Uncle Vern's eyes after the sewer lid fell on him. Everything lurched left, then right, then left again. "Help! Runaway Christmas tree!" cried the cat, just as the tree tipped all the way over.

Fortunately, the tree and I both landed on something soft. Unfortunately for the cat, it was the cat. "Now look what you made me do," he groaned. "When Santa sees this mess, I'll be on his 'naughty' list for life! I'm already on probation, you know."

"Then there's just one thing to do," I said.

"Right! I'll blame it on Odie," said the cat.

"Put the tree back up," I explained. "None of the ornaments are broken. Santa will never know."

"But I can't decorate the top of the tree, rodent. You saw what happened when I tried to climb up there."

"*You* can't climb up there," I replied. "But *I* can . . . on one condition: You let me spend Christmas Eve here."

"Okay, I give in. You can sleep in Jon's stocking."

It wasn't long before the tree was standing and the trimmings were once again in their proper places.

"What should we do now?" I asked, as we sank into an easy chair.

"Let's wait up for Santa," said Garfield. "I want to make sure he brings me everything I asked for."

"What did you ask for?"

"Like I said . . . everything!"

We never did see Santa, but that was okay. Garfield quickly fell asleep. And very soon not a creature was stirring . . . not even a rat.

Merry Christmas!